The Gift of the Willows

For John, who is so much a part of this book.
With thanks to Kenny for planting the seed.

Library of Congress Cataloging-in-Publication Data

Pittman, Helena Clare.
The gift of the willows.

Summary: A Japanese potter and his wife experience
the vicissitudes of the seasons in their home by
the river, as they both give help and receive it
from two willow trees whose tenacity to live symbolize
man's desire to surmount life's obstacles.
[1. Japan—Fiction] I. title.
PZ7.P689Gi   1988   [E]   88-16235
ISBN 0-87614-354-0 (lib. bdg.)
Manufactured in the United States of America

2 3 4 5 6 7 8 9 10 98 97 96 95 94 93 92 91 90 89

The Gift of the Willows

Helena Clare Pittman

Carolrhoda Books, Inc., Minneapolis

Yukiyo Takasama of Shinjo was a potter.
His workshop stood on a hilltop
overlooking the Okayama River on
one side and the sea on the other.
Each morning, as Yukiyo dug his
clay at the river's edge, he imagined
the pots he would make with it. This will be a teapot, he
thought. This a wine bottle.

Back in his shop he worked the clay with his bare
feet to make it smooth and pliable. Then he centered
a lump of clay on the potter's wheel and kicked
to make it spin. He kicked and kicked,
and his feet looked as if they were dancing.
The lump beneath his fingers grew
and changed like magic until there
appeared a perfect oil jar, or flower
vase, or rice dish to bake in the
clay oven until it was as
strong as stone.

Next to Yukiyo's work-
shop stood his rice-paper
house and the pottery shop
with wooden shelves where
his jars and bowls sat waiting
to be bought. All of this Yukiyo
had built with his own hands.
In the evenings, when the moon
rose pink above the sea and the
fragrance of plum blossoms floated
over the hillside, Yukiyo was filled
with contentment.

"Life is good," he would say to the stars. So filled to overflowing was Yukiyo that sometimes he yearned to share his life with someone else.

Then Yukiyo met Kura, the daughter of Mr. Samahira, the rice seller.

He married her, and his happiness was complete.

As if she had always been there, Kura became part of life on the hill. Yukiyo taught her his craft. Soon the windows of the pottery shop were hung with clay chimes and bells that she made, which tinkled sweetly in the winds from the sea. At times she sang softly to Yukiyo, delicately plucking the strings of her koto.

If Yukiyo had been content before, happiness now shone from his face like the morning sun.

"Life is joy," he said softly to the trees.

The days passed. One morning at the river, Yukiyo unloaded the jars from his yoke and set about digging his clay. He scooped the soft, red substance out of the earth and packed his jars until they were full. When he finished, he sat back to rest and to watch the Okayama as it bubbled along its way. Sunlight glanced from the surface of the water and lit sparkling patterns in the leaves of the surrounding trees.

"How beautiful is this place!" said Yukiyo. As he sighed peacefully, his eyes fell upon two willow seedlings growing at the river's edge. They stood straight and proud with their branches already draping gracefully, as if they were full-grown trees. Yukiyo was touched by their dignity, while his heart was moved to pity, for he was sure they would never survive the first rains of spring. But one summer morning, Yukiyo noticed them again, taller and full with leaves. He smiled all the way up the path to his workshop.

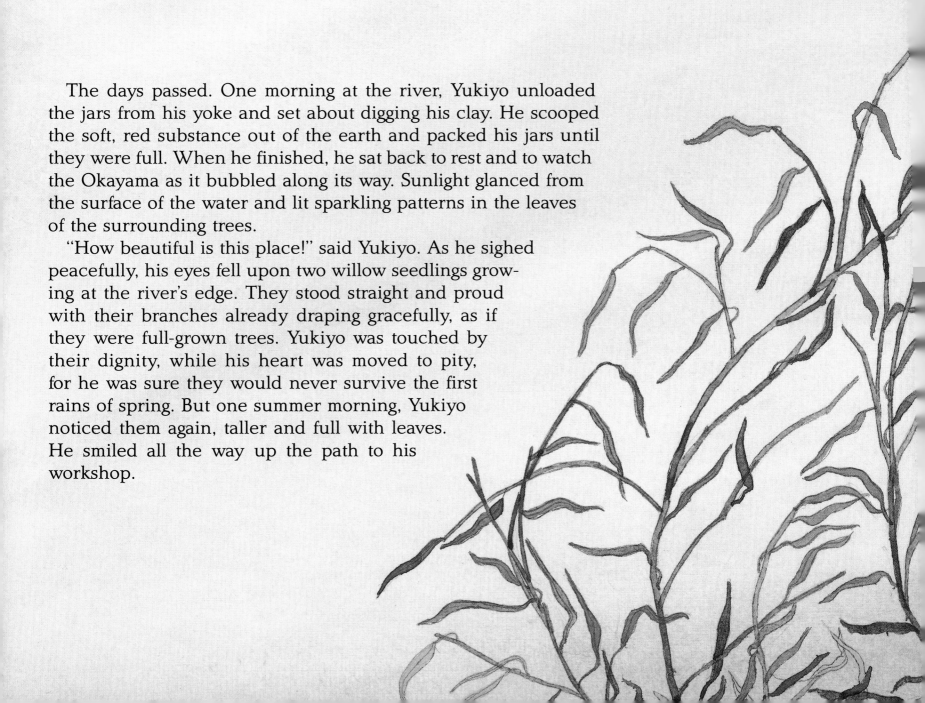

As the months went by, Yukiyo's pottery became more beautiful, and sweeter were the notes of Kura's chimes. So great was their happiness that they yearned to share it. More and more they hoped for a child.

One day in autumn, Yukiyo nearly lost his balance while lifting his yoke. He reached out and caught hold of a sapling to steady himself. Another sapling stood nearby. At once he recognized the willows.

"Still here!" he exclaimed as he pulled himself to his feet. All the way up the hill he marveled at how they had grown. He walked quickly in spite of his heavy load.

Months turned to years. Life on the hill was rich. Season after season, Yukiyo and Kura made teapots and wind chimes, ink trays and water jars, coal boxes and cooking pots, which found their way all over Japan. Each season's wares were finer than the ones before, and word traveled with each pot that a man and his wife in the hills of Shinjo made the finest pottery in all of Japan. Travelers knocked on the door of the shop and asked to see the chimes and bells that were said to tinkle like splintering ice.

Every autumn, leaves from the willows made a soft carpet where Yukiyo sat after digging his clay. Their trunks grew thick and strong; so strong that Yukiyo would settle back against one to let the breeze cool his skin. Sometimes he spoke aloud to the willows thoughts which came from his heart. Now when he went to the river, he greeted the trees as friends.

Time passed, but still no child was born to Yukiyo and Kura. Then one summer the sky turned yellow. The ground became brittle. In the fields the crops died, and rice withered on the stalk. The people of Shinjo prayed for rain, but none fell. Each day Yukiyo knelt on the riverbank digging deeper into the hardened earth for his clay. He watched the fish die. He watched the squirrels grow thin.

The river sank low and became dark and foul. Still Yukiyo and Kura filled their jars from it. Up and down the hill they trudged under the glaring sun, pouring water on their garden to keep it alive. Their meals were made of a bit of stored rice and a few beans.

"Life is hardship,"
Yukiyo sighed to the yellow
moon. With little time to make
pottery, Yukiyo's journeys to the river
for clay were few. He all but forgot
the willow trees. When he noticed them
again, their bare limbs sagged over the
river like the bones of giants, and only
a few withered leaves curled around
their shriveled branches.

Yukiyo was filled with sorrow. He had seen the trees survive the rains of spring, the winds of winter. But if it did not rain soon, they would surely die. Never again would their graceful branches shelter him from the sun. Where would he sit, then, to listen to the lovely melody of the Okayama's song as it sang along its journey to the sea? Who would he greet when he came to dig his clay?

Suddenly hope leapt into Yukiyo's heart. He sprang to his feet and waded into the river. He filled his jar and watered the willows' roots. Slipping on the slimy stones, he flung water high into the branches. He splashed their thick trunks. With his pick he broke up the baked earth to make a trench around both trees. Again and again he filled his jar and emptied it into the dirt until finally the gully held water. The next day Yukiyo did the same thing and all the days after that, until at last the heavens opened and watered the earth.

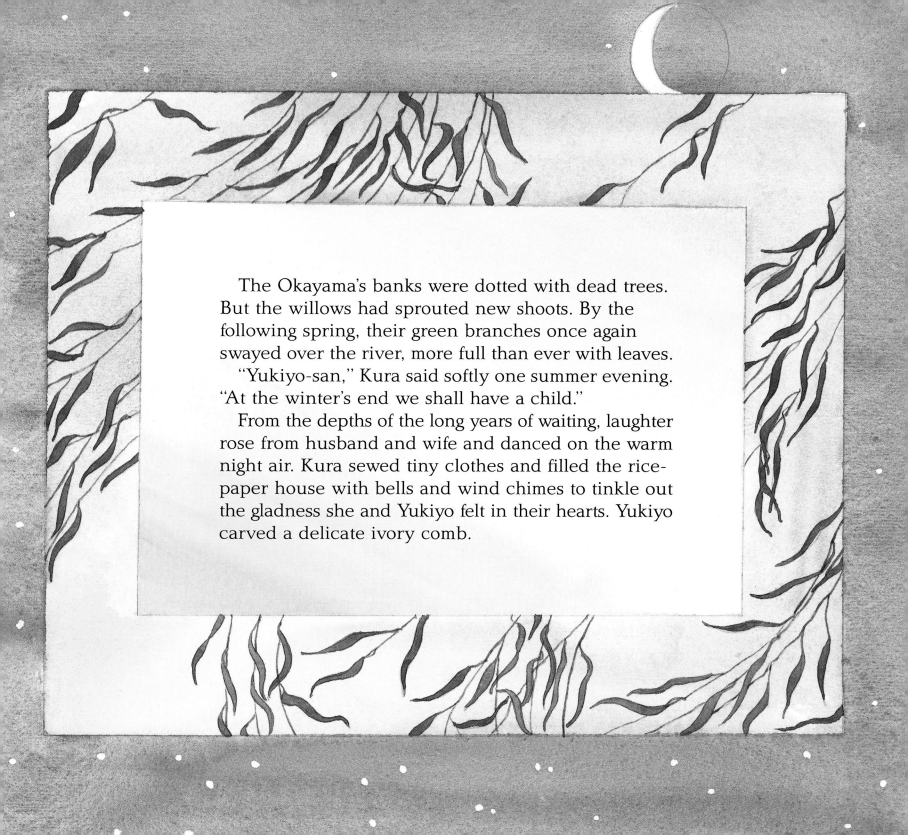

The Okayama's banks were dotted with dead trees.
But the willows had sprouted new shoots. By the
following spring, their green branches once again
swayed over the river, more full than ever with leaves.

"Yukiyo-san," Kura said softly one summer evening.
"At the winter's end we shall have a child."

From the depths of the long years of waiting, laughter
rose from husband and wife and danced on the warm
night air. Kura sewed tiny clothes and filled the rice-
paper house with bells and wind chimes to tinkle out
the gladness she and Yukiyo felt in their hearts. Yukiyo
carved a delicate ivory comb.

All that fall Yukiyo cut wood for the coming winter. When the bitter winds came, they whipped the rice-paper walls. The sea churned, and deep snow drifts buried the hill. One day Yukiyo heard tree limbs crashing into the river. He fought his way through the storm to the top of the hill. Hoping to catch a glimpse of the willows, he looked toward the river. In the place where he knew they stood, he could see only one, bent by the driving wind. When the storm had spent itself, the rice-paper house stood torn and broken. Yukiyo worked night and day to patch the walls so that Kura would be warm.

"Life is struggle," he said to the dull gray sky.

One morning a soft breeze carried the scent of snow drops, and birds announced the coming of spring. Every day the air was warmer, changing the snow to water, which flowed down the hill to the river.

"It is time, husband," Kura said one morning. Yukiyo made his way to Shinjo for the midwife. That night Kutsu was born. He had thick hair and deep, still eyes like Kura's.

Yukiyo lay in the dark and looked at his wife's peaceful face. Above the soft sound of Kutsu's breathing, he heard the melting snow. He heard ice falling from the trees and tumbling into the Okayama River. He lay awake and worried, for he knew that with the thaw would come flooding. If the river rose high enough, everything on the hill could be washed away. There was no question in Yukiyo's mind. They would have to leave.

The next two
days passed slowly.
Yukiyo waited. If they
were to leave safely, Kura and
the baby needed time to grow
stronger. Meanwhile, melting
ice cascaded down the hill.
The Okayama deepened.

On the third day after Kutsu's birth, Yukiyo made his way down to the willows. Only one remained standing. The other was leaning upon it, caught in an embrace of branches, half of its roots ripped from the ground. The river raced around them, out of control.

Yukiyo could smell sap. The life had not yet left the uprooted tree. Tenderly, he touched the tiny buds at the tips of its branches and shook his head.

"So," he said sadly. "You have lived through your last winter."

But the sight of the fallen tree, gnarled and twisted with its seasons, turned Yukiyo's pity to anger, and he raised his voice above the roaring river.

"Why do you do it?" he cried to the willows. "Why do you bloom each year only to lose the struggle against drought and wind and flood?"

At that moment the wind whipped through the willows' branches. "Look how we have grown," they sighed.

Suddenly, just above the workshop, a wall of snow and melting ice gave way. It struck the roof, which collapsed onto the shelves of pottery. Splintered wood and clay shards tumbled down the hill into the raging river. Now Yukiyo could see Kura, with the baby tied to her back, standing in the doorway of the rice-paper house. Yukiyo fought his way up the hill. Kura hurried toward him. At last their hands met, and they held each other fast. Together they struggled to the willows and held on. The river thundered like a crazed giant.

"Husband!" Kura cried. "We cannot go farther."
The river beat against the fallen tree. Suddenly, with a groan, the leaning willow tore loose and crashed across the river to the opposite bank. Yukiyo caught his breath. It made a perfect bridge.

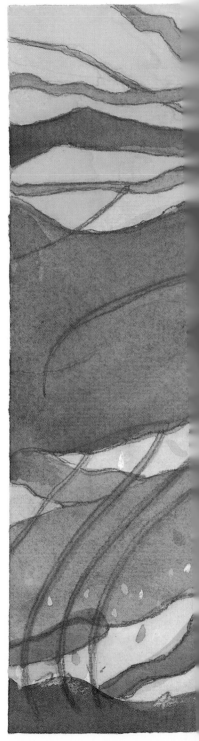

Now he gripped Kura and from branch to branch they pulled themselves across the river. On the other side, the slopes were gentler. They made their way to Shinjo village, where Kura's family sheltered them.

Many days passed before
the flood waters receded and
it was safe to return to the
hill. On their way back,
Yukiyo and Kura spoke
quietly of rebuilding
what they had lost. At
twilight they reached
the river. Debris
lay everywhere, and
the riverbank had so
changed that they hardly
recognized it. But there were the
willows, one standing, the other bridging
the two riverbanks. To Yukiyo's amazement,
the roots of the fallen tree had turned and
embedded themselves firmly into the mud.
Tender green leaves had unfolded along its
branches.

Kura cradled the baby close to her, and she
and Yukiyo looked with awe at the standing
willow. It towered like a vast umbrella fill-
ing the sky. The evening star twinkled
through its branches, and its leaves shim-
mered under the new spring moon.

Yukiyo smiled. How well he
remembered the tiny seedlings
growing at the edge of the river.

"Life is growing," he said
softly to his wife and child.

The Takasama family increased and thrived, while their pottery came to be known all over the world. The living willow bridge remained a place where travelers could safely cross the Okayama River.